祕密池塘

Snapdragon And The Pool

作者：珍奈特・卡樂（Janet Cullup）
譯者：樸慧芳 / 插畫：林俐

高談文化

編者的話

　　當精緻的出書夢想，遇上了精緻的出版理念，會出現什麼樣的組合呢？您所看到的這本書就是在如此的理想結合下孕育而成。

　　高談文化素來堅持精緻出版的理念，無論在重點人物傳記、精緻藝術論叢、深度旅遊探索及英語學習等領域，都有頗受好評的出版成績，當本書作者與我們談及這一系列適合英國兒童閱讀的童話故事時，中英對照的出版靈光乍現於腦海中。

　　我們相信，在欣賞童話故事的同時，也能兼顧英語學習，豈不一舉兩得？而家長在陪同孩子閱讀童話故事之餘，也有練習英語的機會，更能賦予本書不同的功能，使全家大小都一同參與閱讀，讓讀書成為全家共享的一大樂事。

　　<霹靂龍歷險記>的故事主角是一條由一名商人變成的印度巨蟒，天堂的守衛答應給他一次機會，回到人世間完成幫助人的好事之後，才能夠進入天堂，於是這名商人以蛇的身形回到世上，經歷了一連串險象環生的冒險，而每一個冒險故事發人深省之處，都值得你親自去體會。

作者：珍奈特‧卡樂 (Janet Cullup)

　　　　英國劍橋大學教育碩士，詩人及作家

　　　　作品散見英國各報，詩作收錄於英國年度優良詩選輯中多年。

譯者：樸慧芳

　　　　台大中文系畢，具多年編輯經驗，從事英語教學多年，目前為地球村英語中心英教師。

祕密池塘

在一個大城市的郊外，櫻花盛開的動物園裡，住著一隻非常特別的蛇，非常特別！他的名字叫霹靂龍，是一條巨型的印度蟒蛇，人們從各個不同的地方來到這

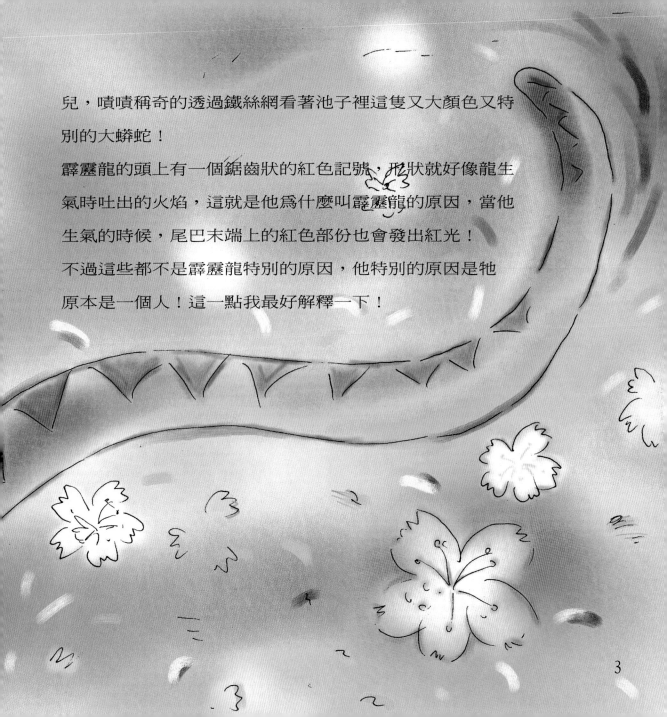

兒，嘖嘖稱奇的透過鐵絲網看著池子裡這隻又大顏色又特別的大蟒蛇！

霹靂龍的頭上有一個鋸齒狀的紅色記號，形狀就好像龍生氣時吐出的火焰，這就是他為什麼叫霹靂龍的原因，當他生氣的時候，尾巴末端上的紅色部份也會發出紅光！

不過這些都不是霹靂龍特別的原因，他特別的原因是牠原本是一個人！這一點我最好解釋一下！

3

霹靂龍原本是一個生意人，但卻是一個不誠實的生意人，他愛金錢勝過一切而且經常欺騙別人，這樣他才可以賺更多的錢。

所以當他離開人世到另一個世界時，天堂的守門人擋住了他的路，嚴厲的說：

「你不能進來，你太愛錢了，除非你了解人比錢更重要的道理，否則就不能進天堂。」

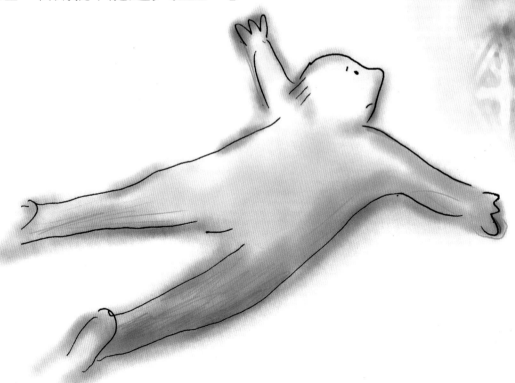

多嚇人啊！這個生意人苦苦地哀求守衛。

「求求你再給我一次機會，我一定會做一個好人的。」他害怕自己永遠都被拒絕在天堂之外。

「好吧！」守衛動了惻隱之心：「但是你必須回到人世，做些無私的好事，改正以往所做的錯事。」

「任何事都好！」這個人說。守衛微笑著說：「我會在你的頭上做個紅色記號，所以無論你到哪裡我都認得出你來。」

這個人猶豫了一會兒，但是他知道自己能有第二次機會已經很幸運了？

「我同意。」他說。守衛接著說：「只要你完成一件好事，我就會在你身旁種一朵永不凋謝的小白花，等開滿了足夠的花時，你就可以進入天堂了。」

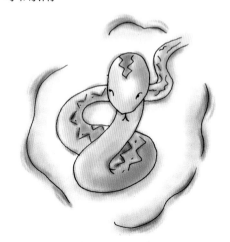

他揮一揮手，這個人就變成了一條蛇，雖然他仍然聽得懂人的話，可是卻只能發出嘶嘶的聲音。

2　霹靂龍發現自己住在一個叢林裡，睡在樹底下，在清澈的
池塘裡，被陽光晒溫的水中洗澡，可是那裡得到小白花的機會並
不多。

有一天，他被抓到動物園，因為他巨大的體型，以及特殊的記號，很快就成為吸引觀光客的明星動物。

在動物園裡負責照顧他的是黛西，她是一個年輕清瘦的女孩，有一頭金色的長髮，要不是她的那頭長髮，一定會被誤認為是男孩，因為她老是把頭髮綁起來藏在帽子裡，工作時也老穿著一件藍色套頭衫。

黛西很喜歡爬蟲類，
而霹靂龍是她的最愛，
每當她送食物給霹靂龍時，
總是撫摸他的下巴問道：
「你今天好不好？我的帥哥！」

9

「我很好啊！」霹靂龍回答，但是聽起來當然只有一長串嘶嘶嘶的聲音。他小心翼翼地把自己捲在她身上，而且不能太用力，因為每個人都知道印度蟒蛇是可以輕易把人捲死的。

霹靂龍絕不會傷害黛西，他只想讓黛西
知道自己有多麼喜歡她，而黛西根
本就不怕他，她和他說話，對著
他唱歌，印度蟒蛇向來就喜歡
音樂，所以當黛西邊聽音樂
邊唱歌時，霹靂龍就跟著
音樂的節奏擺動著身子。

「霹靂龍，你知不知道你眞的很漂亮?」黛西說，她一邊微笑一邊
用手指撥弄霹靂龍頭上的紅色鋸齒記號?

「妳是全動物園裡最漂亮的。」霹靂龍用他
的寬嘴微笑回答，他很高興黛
西這麼喜歡他，不像其他來
動物園參觀的人，只會擠
成一堆，看著他說:
「哦！好可怕啊！」

霹靂龍發現了兩個可以跑出蛇坑的方法，
一個是罩在坑洞的鐵絲網邊邊的一個小
洞，另一個是在坑洞旁被老常春藤蓋住

的廢棄廢棄水管，霹靂龍利用這兩個通道去發掘動物園外的世界。

3　學校放假的第一天，天氣十分炎熱，藍色的天空沒有一朵
雲，太陽似乎要把所有的東西都給燒了，霹靂龍在他的洞穴裡老
常春藤的樹蔭下打盹。

「這裡真的太熱了。」他一邊抱怨一邊睜開一隻眼睛：「現在沒什麼遊客，我想我暫時失蹤一陣子應該沒人會發現，反正他們正忙著看獅子吃東西呢！」抓住一個機會，霹靂龍迅速悄悄的滑到樹後，消失在廢棄的水管裡。

水管裡幾乎沒有足夠的空間讓霹靂龍滑行，他的身體擠滿了整個水管，不過他並不擔心自己會被卡住。

水管在動物園圍牆外搖擺的青草及野花間若隱若現，就在過去一點的地方，樹枝垂在水中劃起陣陣漣漪，潺潺水流滴入清澈見底的池水中，這是個人跡罕至的地方，一個祕密的地方。快到水邊的時候，霹靂龍停住了，因為他發現自己並非一個人，那兒已經有人了，一個小男孩正在水塘邊釣魚，全神貫注的看著水中漂浮的魚線。

　　霹靂龍將自己蜷曲在樹上，想趁不注意的時候鑽進水裡，不過最後他決定：「我看還是別冒險吧！」
過了一會兒，小男孩把漁竿放下，打開一個午餐盒，霹靂龍往前靠近一些，「哦！薯片！」他嘆了一口氣，又吸了一口氣：「酸醋口味，我的最愛！」
霹靂龍實在很懷念人類的食物，尤其是薯片和冰淇淋，於是他又爬近了一些。

突然間，小男孩發現了他！嚇得嘴巴張得大大的，薯片正往嘴裡送到一半，還拿在手裡，但是他沒有尖叫，也沒有跑開。反而問道：「你從動物園逃出來的嗎？要不要來一片？」

他把薯片拿在手中，那實在令人難以拒絕，霹靂龍迅速地一口吞了下去，真是人間美味。

「你聽得懂我說的話，對不對？」小男孩微笑的又給了他另一片。

霹靂龍張開他的寬嘴微笑，把頭低下小心的把薯片送進嘴裡，然後用具彈性的身體捲出自己的名字，「我叫霹靂龍，你叫什麼?」

男孩十分吃驚的說：「麥可，我叫麥可，你...你是真的蛇嗎?我真不敢相信我在跟一條蛇說話，等一下，我去告訴我朋友!」

霹靂龍把蛇尾尖端放在嘴巴前：「不!別告訴別人，這是個祕密。」麥可弄懂他的意思了：「沒問題! 我答應你絕不告訴任何人。」

一陣「ㄨㄧ，ㄨㄧ，ㄨㄧ」的聲響讓他不禁回頭，漁線在水中拖出一條長長的水痕。「我釣到了，我釣到了。」他興高采烈的大叫，同時死命把漁竿往後拉。

「一定是一條大魚。」他氣喘吁吁咬牙收捲著漁線，慢慢把漁線往裡捲。

霹靂龍看見水面下的銀色陰影突然
一翻身，扭過漁線把男孩一個
倒栽蔥拖進了水裡。
「哦！糟了！」霹靂龍嘶嘶叫著，
迅速鑽進波紋漣漣的冷水中。

21

4　霹靂龍一直往下游，往下游，
游到麥可的腰部，長長的
尾巴在水裡捲起像個
大大的漩渦，把
男孩輕輕捲住。

好不容易游出水面，霹靂龍才鬆了一口氣，他把尾巴
當成船舵，急速划向岸邊，男孩的眼睛閉得緊緊的，
身體一點力氣也沒有，

霹靂龍輕輕的把男孩拖到岸邊的草地
上，面朝下的把他放下。

男孩一動也不動，霹靂龍不禁嘶嘶地叫著：「這下可嚴重了！」
於是他用身體捲住男孩的胸口，並且有規律的壓擠著，

一次，

二次，

三次，

然後停下來看看有沒有生命的跡象。

「快！麥可，張開眼睛，還有好多魚等你去抓呢！」

霹靂龍一次又一次用身體擠壓著男孩，小心的壓擠，突然間男孩
開始咳嗽，霹靂龍鬆了一口氣，發出一陣嘶嘶聲，

麥可的嘴裡因為開口說話而潰出水來，他動了動
頭，睜開眼睛坐了起來，瞪大眼睛出神的看著捲在
一旁的霹靂龍。

霹靂龍露出大大的寬嘴微笑著說：「感謝老天！」然後搖搖紅尾巴，消失在高高的草叢中，往動物園的路走去。

「喂！等一下！等等！回來啊！」霹靂龍聽到麥可的
叫聲隨著微風拂動青草的聲音傳來，但他直到返
回安全的坑洞之前並沒有停下來。
「哎呀！可把我累壞了！」他自言自語的嘆了口
氣，閉上雙眼纏繞在老常春藤的樹幹上。

5「就是他！爸爸，我知道就是他！」霹靂龍聽到聲音後立刻驚慌的睜開了眼睛，「哦！不！」他馬上又閉上眼睛假裝睡覺，在還沒看到麥可前，這個從祕密池塘被救回來的男孩，就已經指著霹靂龍對著身旁的高個子又叫又跳的。

那個男人朝下望著霹靂龍，露出一臉不相信的樣子：「別傻了！麥可，那不過是條蛇罷了。」

「可是，就是他啊！爸爸，我知道是他，我看到他了。」麥可似乎很想讓這個男人相信他所說的一切。

「而且，爸爸，一般蟒蛇的頭上不會有鋸齒形的記號，所以我認得他，這條蛇很特別的⋯」麥可耐心的解釋。

「麥可，我看你是掉進池塘裡把腦子碰壞了！」爸爸回答他說：「要不就是你在太陽下曬太久了！」

男孩深深吸了一口氣，想再次說服爸爸；「爸爸，你不懂啦！是他把我從水裡拖出來的，我原本想游上岸，可是我的衣服裡都是水，根本游不動，而且池塘太深了，是他救了我，他是個英雄！⋯」

「麥可！」父親的聲音透露著警告，認為男孩太離譜了：「你說的根本就不可能發生，這條蛇在這個深洞裡，根本不可能跑出去，就算他有足夠的力氣，我也很懷疑。」小男孩還是不願放棄；「爸爸，他一定是⋯」

「夠了，麥可！你捏造這件事只是想讓我忘了你根本不應該到池塘邊玩，而且還把漁竿弄丟、把衣服弄髒。」

他停了一下，在小男孩還來不及打斷之前補充一句：「在我還沒有真正生氣之前趕快回家！晚餐時間到了，媽媽已經在等我們了。」

就這樣，爸爸把抗議的男孩抓了回去，霹靂龍也鬆了一口氣。「感謝老天，大人只相信自己眼睛所看到的，他們總認為小孩子想像力太豐富了。」霹靂龍閉著眼睛想。

6 當黛西餵霹靂龍吃晚餐時，不禁疑惑的看著被老常春藤覆蓋

著的樹。

「那是什麼時候跑出來的?」她大喊：「我確定早上的時候樹上並

沒有這個東西啊！」

霹靂龍張開眼睛看了看，然後露出慣有的寬嘴笑得開開
的，黛西張大著嘴瞪著大樹頂端，看起來真好笑。

在那高高的樹葉之間，他看到一朵從沒見過的美麗純白花朵，花瓣正慢慢的展開著。

「你知道這是怎麼一回事嗎?」黛西問霹靂龍，一如往常，只問他問題並不期待他的答案。

「我當然知道!」霹靂龍點點頭；「總有一天我會告訴妳我的祕密，但不是現在。」

突然間，霹靂龍看見麥可從繞著坑洞的鐵絲網外看著他，眼神看來似乎要做出什麼令人意外的事似的。

但是，麥可手裡拿著一袋薯片，一句話也不說地，遞給霹靂龍吃。

「嘿！你在幹什麼？」黛西阻止道：「你難道不知道蛇不吃薯片的嗎？」

「但是這一條吃！」麥可微笑著回答，這時霹靂龍已自己從袋子裡拿出薯片自己享用了起來。

「別擔心，」麥可小聲的說：「我會保守你的祕密，很抱歉之前我忘了，但這次我保證絕不會告訴任何人的。」霹靂龍保留了這些薯片，滿足的看了一眼白色的小花。

「嗯！」他喃喃自語：「達成了一件，不知還要幾件才能完成我的任務。」

當然別人聽起來，不過只是一連串的嘶嘶聲，畢竟，霹靂龍只是一條蛇，但卻是多特別的蛇啊！

Snapdragon And The Pool

The snake that lives in the deep pit of the cherry blossom zoo on the out skirts of a large city is special! Very special.

His name is Snapdragon and he is an enormous Indian Python.

44

People come from far and wide to look over the top
and through the wire sides of his pit just to watch him,
amazed at the size of him and fascinated by his unusual
coloring.

Snapdragon has red zig zag marks on his head, similar
to the flames dragons breathe out when they are annoyed.
This is why he is named Snapdragon and the red tip of
his tail also glows when he is annoyed about
something.

None of these are the reasons why Snapdragon is special. He
is special because he is, or rather was, a man! Perhaps I had
better explain.

When Snapdragon lived in the world of men he was a businessman. But he was also dishonest. He loved money more than anything and often cheated people so he could make even more money.

So, when he finally reached the world that exists beyond ours he found the Guardian at the gates of Paradise barring his way.

"You cannot enter here," he said sternly.

"You love money more than anything. People are more important than money and until you realize that you can never enter Paradise."

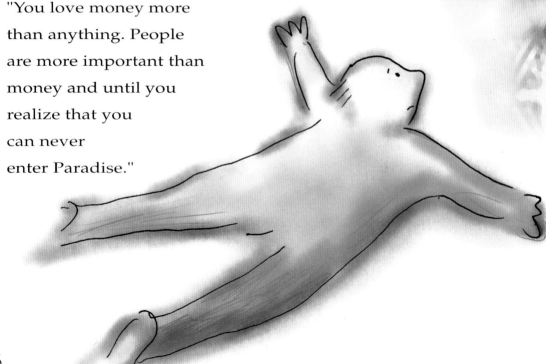

What a shock! The business man pleaded with the Guardian.

"Please, please give me another chance and I will try to be a better person." He was frightened at the thought of being locked out of Paradise forever.

"Very well," replied the Guardian relenting. "But you must return to your world and make amends for all the wrong things you have done by doing some unselfish deeds."

"Anything, anything," said the man. The Guardian smiled, "Don't be hasty, you must return as a snake and I will place a red mark on your head so I can recognize you anywhere you go."

The man hesitated, but only for a moment, he knew he was lucky to get a second chance.

"I agree," he said.

"I promise," the Guardian added, "that for every good deed you complete I will create an everlasting white flower to bloom wherever you are in the world. When there are enough flowers blooming I will allow you into Paradise."

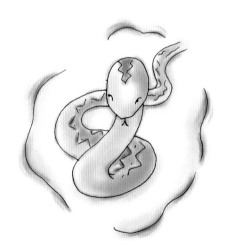

2 With a wave of his hand, the man was transformed into a snake, retaining the ability to understand human speech but only able to hiss. Snapdragon found himself living in the jungle and for a while he slept beneath trees and bathed in pools of clear water warmed by the sun. But there were few opportunities to earn white flowers there.

Then, one day, he was captured and brought to the zoo where his size and unusual markings made him a star attraction.

His keeper at the zoo was called Daisy. She was young and slim, with long, fair hair. If it had not been for her hair, she might easily have been mistaken for a boy because she always pushed it up under a cap and wore dark blue overalls when she worked.

Daisy loved reptiles and Snapdragon was her special favorite. She tickled him under his chin when she brought his food and always asked. "How are you today my handsome man?"

51

"I'm fine," Snapdragon answered, but of course it sounded like one long hiss. He wound himself around her affectionately taking care not to hug too tightly because as everyone knows Pythons can squeeze people to death.

Snapdragon would never hurt Daisy, he only wanted to show how much he liked her. She was never afraid of him. She talked to him and sang him songs. Pythons are very fond of music and Snapdragon swayed in time to the music when Daisy had her radio on.

"You know you really are very beautiful Snapdragon." Daisy said, smiling as she traced her finger along the red zig zag on his head.

"And I think you are the most beautiful keeper in the zoo," Snapdragon replied with his wide, wide snake smile. He was glad Daisy loved him, not like the visitors to the zoo who crowded around murmuring, "Ugh, how horrible," as they gazed down at him.

Snapdragon had discovered two ways to escape from his pit. One was through a small hole in the corner of the wire that covered the top of his pit. The other was through a long forgotten, old disused pipe hidden behind the old ivy covered tree that

grew to one side of his pit. Using these escape
routes Snapdragon was
able to explore the
outside world as
well as the zoo.

3 The first day of the school holidays came and it was very , very hot. Not a cloud in the clear blue sky and the sun seemed to burn everything it touched. Snapdrag onlay dozing in the shade of the old ivy covered tree in his pit.

As it grew even hotter, Snapdragon thought of the cool, blue pool filled by a waterfall that he had discovered beyond the wall of the zoo wall and he longed to be there.

"It's too hot here," he complained, opening one eye to look around."There's not many visitors today, I'm sure no one will miss me for a while. Anyway, they are too busy watching the lions being fed." he hissed.

Seizing his chance, Snapdragon slithered swiftly andsilently behind the tree and disappearedinto the black darknessof the disused pipe.

Inside the pipe there was barely enough room for Snapdragon to slide along and his muscular body almost filled the pipe, but he refused to worry about getting stuck.

The pipe emerged among tall waving grasses and wild flowers beyond the walls that surrounded the zoo. A little further on, beneath trees which trailed their branches in it`s rippling waters a fast running stream dropped down into a crystal clear pool that few people had discovered. This was a secret place.

Reaching the edge of the water, Snapdragon stopped and stared. He was not alone. Somebody was already there! A young boy was fishing in the deep pool concentrating as he watched his float bobbing on the surface of the water.

Snapdragon coiled himself around a tree and wondered if he could slide unnoticed into the water. "No," he decided, "I'd better not risk it."
A moment later the boy put down his fishing rod and opened a small lunch box. Snapdragon slid closer. "Ah, Crissspsss," he sighed longingly, sniffing the air. "Sssalt and vinegar, my favorite!"

Snapdragon missed the taste of human food, especially crisps and ice cream.
He slithered even nearer.

59

Suddenly the boy saw him! His mouth dropped open in amazement , a crisp still in his hand halfway to his mouth, but he didn't scream or run away.

"Have you escaped from the zoo?" he asked, then, "Would you like a crisp?"

He held out the crisp in his hand and it was irresistible. Quickly Snapdragon took it and swallowed. It tasted absolutely divine.

"Hey, you understood what I said, didn't you!" The boy smiled and offered Snapdragon another crisp.

Snapdragon smiled his wide, wide snake smile, lowered his head and carefully took the crisp with his mouth. Then he twisted his flexible body to spelled out, "My name is Snapdragon, what's yours?"

The child stared, then said, "Michael, my name is Michael, but...but...are you real? I can't believe I'm really talking to a snake! Wait till I tell my friends!"

Snapdragon put the tip of his tail to his mouth, "No! Don't tell anyone!" he hissed. "It'sss a sssecret!"

Michael understood, "It's O.K. I won't tell anyone! I promise!"

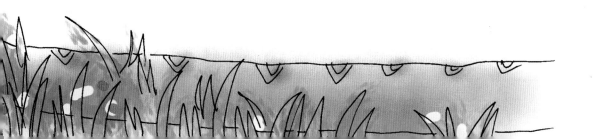

Then a loud "Wheeee," made him look round. The line was pulling from his fishing reel way out across the water.

"I've got one! I've got one!" Shouting jubilantly he snatched up his rod and pulled it backwards as hard as he could.

"It must be a big one," he gasped
as the line raced away.
Gritting his teeth
he wound the reel
furiously, slowly
pulling the
line towards
him.

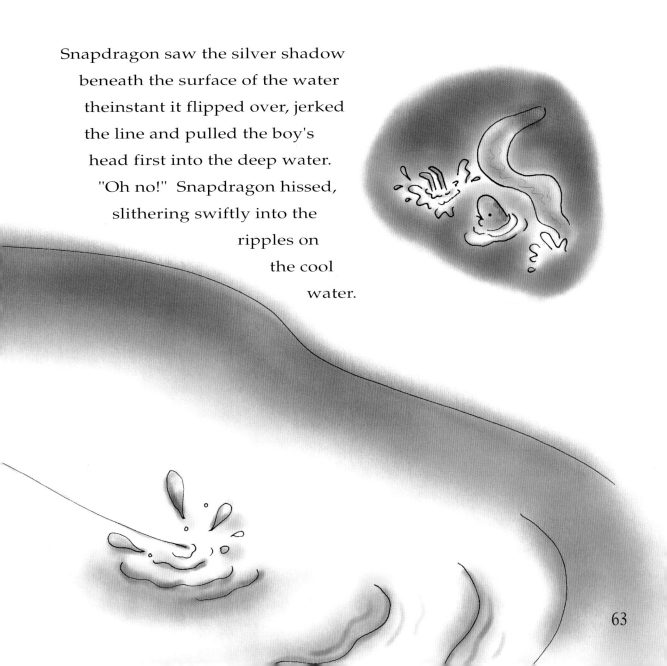

Snapdragon saw the silver shadow
beneath the surface of the water
theinstant it flipped over, jerked
the line and pulled the boy's
head first into the deep water.
"Oh no!" Snapdragon hissed,
slithering swiftly into the
ripples on
the cool
water.

4 Down, down, down he swam
to Michael's waist and with
one gigantic flick of his long
tail shot upwards like a
corkscrew through the
water taking the
child with him.

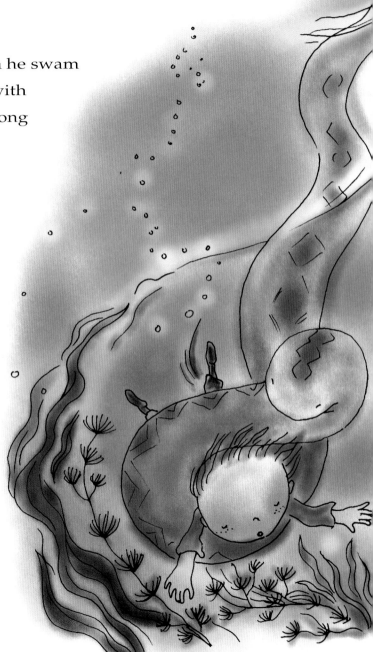

As he burst into the open air, Snapdragon gasped with relief and use his tail like the rudder of a boat splashing it on the water to propel him at speed towards the bank.

The child's eyes were closed and his body limp as Snapdragon gently lifted him onto the grassy bank, lying him face down.

When the child didn't move, Snapdragon hissed, "This is serious," He coiled himself around the boy's chest and squeezed steadily,

once,

twice,

three times.

"Come on Michael!" he urged, "Open your eyes, there are lots more fish for you to catch!"

Again and again Snapdragon coiled himself around the child and gently squeezed.

Suddenly the child coughed and Snapdragon let out a long "hisss" of relief as Michael spluttered water from his mouth, moved his head,
opened his eyes and sat up, staring in amazement at the huge snake coiled beside him.

Snapdragon smiled his wide, wide, snake smile. "Thank goodness," he hissed. Then with a wave of his red tipped tail, disappeared into the tall whispering grasses on his way back to the zoo.

"Hey! Wait a moment! Wait! Come back!"
Snapdragon heard Michael calling him, his
voice carried on the breeze that brushed the
tall waving grasses. But he didn't stop until he
reached the safety of his pit.

"Phew, that was exhausting!" he told himself
with a sigh as he coiled around the trunk of his
old ivy covered tree and closed his eyes.

5 "That's him! Dad that's him! I know that's the one!" Snapdragon opened hie eyes with shock as he recognized the voice.

"Oh no!" he hissed and promptly closed them again pretending to be asleep. But not before he'd seen Michael, the little boy he had pulled from the secret pool jumping up and down with excitement as he pointed Snapdragon out to the tall man beside him.

The man stared down at Snapdragon with undisguised disbelief. "Don't be so silly Michael! It's only a snake!"

"But it is him Dad! I know it is! I saw him!" Michael seemed to be willing the man to believe him.

"Anyway Dad," he explained patiently. "Ordinary Pythons don't have that zigzag on their heads. That's how I recognize him, this snake is special, he...."

"I think you must have hit your head when you fell into the pool Michael" his father replied. "Either that or you've sat too long in the hot sun!"

The child took a deep breath and tried again. "Dad, you don't understand. He pulled me from the water. I was trying to swim but my clothes filled with water and I couldn't , anyway it was too deep. He saved me! He's a hero! He...."

"Michael!" The note of his father's voice warned the child that he was going too far. "What you are saying just isn't possible! This snake is in a deep pit and there is no way, even if it had enough energy, which I doubt, that it could possibly get from here to the pool!"

The child refused to give up, " Dad, he must have somehow...."

"No Michael! You're making it up hoping I'll forget that you are not supposed to go to that pool anyway! And not only did you lose your fishing rod but you also ruined your clothes!"

He paused for breath and before the child could interrupt again added. "Now come along home before I get really cross! It's time for dinner and your mother will be waiting for us!"

With that, the man dragged away the protesting child and Snapdragon breathed a sigh of relief.

"Thank goodness grown ups only believe what they see for themselves and think all
children have vivid
imaginations,
" he hissed
and closed
his eyes.

6 When Daisy brought his supper as usual she stared hard at the old ivy covered tree.

"Where on earth did that come from?" she exclaimed, "It certainly wasn't there this morning."

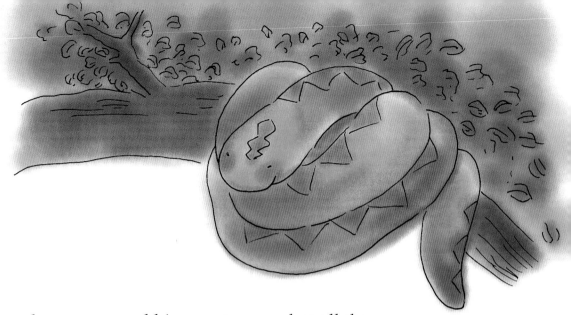

Snapdragon opened his eyes to see what all the
commotion was about and smiled his wide,
wide most innocent snake smile.

Daisy looked so funny with her mouth

wide open in surprise

staring up

at the old ivy

covered tree.

There, high up between the leaves, it's petals slowly unfolding to perfection was the most beautiful pure white flower he had ever seen.

"Do you know anything about this?" Daisy asked Snapdragon. She often addressed questions to him without expecting an answer.

" Yes, I do!" Snapdragon hissed. "And one day I'll tell you my secret-but not yet!"

Suddenly, Snapdragon saw Michael looking at him through the wire that surrounded his pit and for one awful moment thought he was about to let the cat out of the bag.

Instead, Michael held out a bag of crisps and without a word offered them to Snapdragon.

"Hey, what do you think you're doing? "Daisy protested. "Don't you knowsnakes don't eat crisps!"

"This one does,"
Michael replied with a smile as Snapdragon helped himself to the packet.

"Don't worry," Michael whispered. "You're secret is safe with me. Sorry I forgot before, but this time I won't tell anyone, I promise!"

Snapdragons saved the crisps and glanced up with a satisfied sigh at the white flower. "Ah, well," he murmured, "One down, I wonder how many to go."

Of course all that anybody heard if they happened to be listening was a long, long "SSSSSSS," because after all, Snapdragon was only a snake-but what a snake!

霹靂龍（1）
單字解析：

1.

cherry blossom(n.) 櫻花盛開

1. 果樹的花。

例句：apple blossoms蘋果花

2. 開花時期。

例句：come into blossom

　　　進入開花期；

　　　a cherry tree in full blossom 盛開的櫻花樹。

enormous (a.) 巨大的；龐大的

例句：The rent and cost of such a building are enormous.

　　　這棟房子的租金及花費十分龐大。

　　　An enormous nose.

　　　大鼻子。

Indian Python(n.) 印度巨型蟒蛇

fascinated (vt.) 使著迷；使迷惑。

例句：The visitors were fascinated by the flowers in his garden.

訪客被他花園中的花給迷住了。

She is fascinated by Indian culture.
她被印度文化所吸引。

zig zag (n.) 鋸齒狀

dishonest (a.) 不誠實的；不正直的。

例句：He got his money in dishonest way.
他以不誠實的方法獲得金錢。

cheat (vt.) 欺騙

例句：He cheated me of my money.
他騙了我的錢。

guardian(n.) 守衛；保護者；監護人。

例句：A pastor is considered a guardian of faith.
牧師是信仰的護衛者。
The guardian of the gates of Paradise.
天堂之門的守衛。

paradise(n.) 天堂，樂土。

例句：children's paradise

兒童的天堂樂園
shopper's paradise

購物者的天堂
holiday paradise

度假樂土

本書中這個字用大寫，表示是真正人死後會去的天堂。

plead (v.) 辯護；抗辯。

例句：You'd better get a lawyer to plead your case.

你最好找個律師為你的案子辯護。

frighten (vt.) 使吃驚；驚嚇。

例句：The large dog frightened me.

那隻大狗嚇壞了我。

She was frightened to death.

她被嚇得半死。

unselfish (a.) 無私的；不為自己的。

例句：He is a brave and unselfish man.

他是個勇敢無私的人。

That's really an unselfish act.

那真是無私的義舉。

recognize(v.) a). 承認；認可。b.) 認出；認得

例句：He is recognized to be one of the greatest actors of the
20th century.

他被公認為二十世紀最偉大的演員。

You have changed so much that I can hardly recognize you.

你變了這麼多我幾乎認不出你來。

everlasting (a.) 恒久的；耐久的；不朽的。

例句： He believes in everlasting life.
他相信永生。
The everlasting beauty of nature.
大自然永恆之美。

transform (vt.) 使變形；變化外貌。

例句： A tadpole transforms into a frog.
蝌蚪變成了青蛙。
Joy transformed her face.
喜悅改變了她的容貌。

retain(vt.) 保持；維持；保留。

例句： He retains a clear memory of his childhood.
他對童年的記憶猶新。
She retains the innocence of a young girl.
她維持著小女孩般的天真無邪。

2.

jungle (n.) 叢林

例句： The city is a jungle where no one is safe after dark.
這城市猶如一座叢林，入夜後十分不安全。

opportunity(n.) 機會

例句： I won't have an opportunity to make the trip this month.
我這個月沒機會旅行。

Will you have an opportunity to see him?
你有機會見到他嗎？

capture(vt.) 捕獲；捕捉。

例句： Tom captured most of the prizes at school.
湯姆獲得了學校裡大部份的獎品。
The dog was captured by these boys.
這隻狗被這些男孩給捉住了。

attraction(n.) 吸引(力)；誘惑。

例句： A zoo holds great attraction for children.
動物園對小孩子有極大的吸引力。
Mu-Cha Zoo is one of the tourist attractions in Taipei.
木柵動物園是台北的一處觀光勝地。

reptile (n.) 爬蟲類動物

例句： The Indian Python is a reptile.
印度巨蟒是爬蟲類。

favorite(n.) (a.) 喜愛；偏愛

例句： That song is a great favorite of mine.
那首歌是我的最愛。
Ice cream is my favorite food.
我最喜歡的食物是冰淇淋。

affectionately (adv.) 情深的；摯愛的

例句：She looked at him affectionately.
她深情地看著他。

horrible(a.) 可怕的；令人毛骨悚然的。

例句：The horrible story frightened us.
這個可怕的故事嚇壞了我們。

discover(v.) 發現

例句：They discovered a new lake.
他們發現了一個新的湖。

escape(v.) 逃走；逃避

例句：The thief escaped from the police station.
小偷從警察局逃了出來。

explore (v.) 探究；探險

例句：They decided to explore the original forest.
他們決定去原始森林探險。

3.

dozing (doze)(v.) 打盹

例句：The old lady dozed in her armchair.
這位老婆婆在椅子上打盹。

例句：He is dozing over his newspapers.

他看著報紙就打起盹兒來了。

complain(v.) 抱怨

例句： Our neighbor complained about the noise.
咱們的鄰居已經在抱怨噪音了。

slither(v.) 滑行

例句： The snake slithered into the weeds.
蛇滑進了草叢。

disappear(v.) 消失

例句： Where can my keys have disappeared to?
我的鑰匙不見了，會到哪兒去呢？

muscular(adj.) 強壯的，有肌肉的

例句： He is big and muscular.
他既高大又強壯。

stream(n.) 小溪流

例句： There is a stream behind our school.
我們學校後面有條小溪。

crystal(adj. n.) 清澈的; 水晶

例句： This glass is as clear as crystal.
這塊玻璃像水晶一樣透明。

concentrate(v.) 集中; 專心; 濃縮

例句: The student cannot concentrate on the exercise.
學生不能專心做練習。

例句: I don't like concentrated fruit juice, I like fresh juice.
我不喜歡濃縮果汁，我喜歡新鮮的水果。

surface(n.) 表面

例句: A mirror has a smooth surface.
鏡子有光滑的表面。

sniff(v.) 吸氣，吸入

例句: That dog was sniffing for food.
那隻狗正在嗅著找吃的。

amazement(n.) 驚嚇；訝異

例句: He looked at me in amazement.
他驚奇地看著我。

irresistible(adj.) 無法抗拒的

例句: That cate looks irresistible.Please give me a piece.
那蛋糕看起來真令人難以抗拒，請給我一塊。

absolutely(adv.) 絕對地；完全的

例句: He is absolutely wrong.
他完全錯了。

例句: It is absolutely the best show in town.

這無疑是全鎮最棒的演出。

flexible(adj.) 可通融的，有彈性的
例句：My schedule is flexible.
我的行程很有彈性。

promise(v.) 允諾，保證
例句：She promised to lend me her English dictionary.
她答應要借我她的英文字典。

jubilantly(adv.) 喜氣洋洋地
例句：They shouted jubilantly because the won the prize.
他們因爲得獎而喜氣洋洋地歡呼。

snatch(v.) 一把抓住，奪取
例句：The thief snatched her handbag and ran away.
小偷一把搶了她的袋子後跑走了。
例句：The wind snatched her hat off.
風一下子颳走了她的帽子。

backwards(adv.) 往後, 倒轉
例句：It is not easy to walk backwards.
倒著走路不容易。
例句：He drove backwards up the driveway.

他沿著車道倒車。

furiously(adj.) 狂暴地; 猛烈地, 比較常用到的是

例句：He was furious to hear about it.
　　　他聽到這事後十分憤怒。

例句：He kicked the wall furiously.
　　　他狂暴地踢著牆壁。

4.

gigantic(adj.) 巨大的，龐大的

例句：We made a gigantic mistake yesterday.
　　　我們昨天犯了極大的錯誤。

例句：He doesn't look strong but actually has gigantic strength.
　　　他看起來不太強壯，卻有巨大的力量。

corkscrew(n.) 香檳開塞器

例句：Please bring me the corkscrew. I want to open the wine.
　　　幫我把開塞器拿來，我要開這瓶酒。

relief(n.) 寬慰

例句：Your are safe! What a relief!
　　　你平安無事，這樣大家就放心啦！

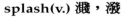

splash(v.) 濺，潑

例句：He splashed water over me.
他把水潑到我身上。

例句：A passing car splashed my dress.
一輛經過的車把水濺在我的洋裝上。

splutter(v.) 噴濺；噴濺唾沫或食物

例句：The ketchup spluttered out of the bottle and made a terrible mess.
番茄醬從瓶中噴出來。

whisper(v.n.) 低語，耳語

例句：The leaves whispered in the breeze.
樹葉在微風中沙沙作響。

例句：The two guests are talking in a whisper.
這兩個人在低聲耳語。

breeze(n.) 微風

例句：There is not much breeze today.
今天幾乎無風。

exhausting(adj.)精疲力盡的

例句：We were exhausting after the three-hour exercise.
三個小時的運動過後令我們精疲力盡。

5.

pretend(v.) 假裝

例句： He pretended he was innocent.
      他假裝自己是無辜的。

例句： She pretended to be sick.
      她裝病。

excitement(n.) 興奮; 刺激

例句： They shouted aloud in excitement.
      他們大聲叫了起來。

例句： The visiting circus was a great excitement.
      來做短期演出的馬戲團令人感到很興奮。

undisguised(adj.) 坦白的; 毫無偽裝的

例句： He looked at her with undisguised disgust.
      他以不加掩飾的嫌惡看著她。

disbelief(n.) 不信任; 疑惑

例句： His disbelief in my ability is obvious.
      他對我的能力懷疑是很明顯的。

ordinary(adj.) 普通的; 一般的

例句： John is just an ordinary policeman.
      約翰只是一位平凡的警察。

interrupt(v.) 中斷; 干擾; 妨礙

例句: Could I interrupt your conversation for a moment?
　　　 我可以打擾一下你們的談話嗎？

protest(v.) 抗議; 反對

例句: Tom protested that he was innocent.
　　　 湯姆抗議他是無罪的。

grown-up(n.) 成人; 大人

例句: Johnny has become a grown-up.
　　　 強尼已經長大成人了。

imagination(n.) 想像力

例句: He is a writer with a rich imagination.
　　　 他是個想像力豐富的作者。

例句: No one moved in the bushes, it was only your imagination.
　　　 沒人在草叢中走動，只不過是你的幻覺罷了。

6.

exclaim(v.) 大聲喊叫; 大聲責罵

例句: "Stop ！Thief" he exclaimed .
　　　 別跑！小偷！他大叫。

例句: He exclaimed that he was hungry.
　　　 他叫喊說肚子餓了。

commotion(n.) 動搖; 騷亂

例句：They were awakened by the commotion in the street.
他們被街上的喧鬧吵醒了。

innocent(adj.) 天眞的; 無罪的

例句：The girl who is talking to the teacher is very innocent.
那個正在跟老師說話的女孩很天眞。

surprise(n.v.) 驚奇; 使人驚嚇

例句：What a surprise！
多麼令人震驚的事！

例句：This, of course, surprised us all.
這自然使我們都很驚奇。

perfection(n.) 完全; 完美

例句：The perfection of our plans will take another week.
我們的計劃還要有一星期才完成。

例句：Perfection in a dictionary is rare.
字典要十全十美是很難得的。

satisfy (v.) 使滿意; 使滿足

例句：Some people are very difficult to satisfy.
有些人很難討好。

例句：I was satisfied with the service of that restaurant.
我對那家餐廳的服務很滿意。

片語解析：

1. sound like 聽起來像

like在此不當作喜歡，而是好像的意思。例如：look like, sound like, taste like, feel like, smell like 等，用於感官動詞之後，表示和熟悉的事物有相類似感覺。

2. afraid of 害怕; 擔心

afraid of + N表示對某件事或某個東西很害怕。

3. fond of 喜歡某事; 對某事感興趣

4. as .. as he could 盡力而爲，有時也用as .. as possible

5. come on 一般用在祈使語，有趕快、來吧、請啦、好啦等意思，爲慫恿或鼓勵人做某事的常用語。

6. thank goodness 謝天謝地！

7. jump up and down 跳上跳下

8.give up 放棄 ;停止

98

文法解析：

1. had better 應該，還是…好，最好…..

一般用於建議時，後面通常接原形動詞

例句：We had better be off.
　　　我們該走了。

例句：You had better not say that.
　　　那樣的話你還是別說的好。

2. make amends for 賠償；補償

爲所做的事做出賠償，介系詞需用for，注意amends 是名詞而非動詞的amend

　　You should make, amends for what you have done.
　　你得爲所作的事付出代價。

3. Don't be hasty 別性急、草率

Don't be + Adj. 爲常用的一種祈使句，後接形容詞。

例句：Don't be afraid !

　　　別害怕 !
　　　Don't be so rude !

　　　別這麼粗魯 !

Don't + V 是另一種常用的祈使句，後接動詞。

例句：Don't worry !

　　　別擔心 !
　　　Don't do that !

　　　別這麼作 !

4.If it had not been---,she might have been 如果沒那麼做….就可能….

這樣的句型在文法中稱爲「和過去事實相反的假設語氣」，if 後接過去完成式，另一子句則是 would/might ＋ 現在完成式

　例句： If it had not been raining, she might have been killed by
　　　　 the fire.
　　　　 如果不是因爲下雨，她可能就因那場火而喪命。

5.as well as 和；除..外也

　在 as well as 前後的兩件事必須是對等的
　例句： He gave me clothes as well as food.
　　　　 他除了食物之外，也給我們衣服。
　例句： He would like to go as well as you.
　　　　 他和你一樣想去。
　clothes 和 food 同樣是日用品，he 和 you 同樣是人稱代名詞

6.seem to 似乎；彷彿覺得

　to 後要接原形動詞或人稱代名詞的受格(me，you，him…)
　例句： It seems good to me to do so.
　　　　 這樣子做似乎不錯。
　例句： I don't seem to like him.
　　　　 我覺得不太喜歡他。

7.wonder if 不知道是否..

除了if之外，也可用 whether,what,who,why…等
疑問詞
例句： I wonder if I can open the window.
　　　　 我不知道可不可以開窗戶。

8. even if 即使；縱使

也可以用 even though

例句：I'll come even if it rains.
　　　即使下兩我也會來。

例句：I shan't mind even if she doesn't come.
　　　即使她不來，我也不介意。

9. The most ---I have ever　我…過最….的

The most 是形容詞的最高級，I have ever +過去分詞，是我.. 過的

例句：She is the most beautiful girl I have ever seen.
　　　她是我見過最漂亮的女孩。

例句：This is the most delicious food I have ever had.
　　　這是我吃過最好吃的食物

國家圖書館出版品預行編目資料

祕密池塘＝The Pool／珍奈特・卡樂
（Janet Cullup）作：樸慧芳譯 . --初
版 . --台北縣新店市：高談文化 . 民89
　面　　公分 . --（霹靂龍歷險記：1）
中英對照
ISBN　957-0443-06-5（精裝）

　　　873.95　　　　　　　　　89012984

89年10月1日 初版
發行人：賴任辰
社 長/總編輯：許麗雯
主　編：樸慧芳
編　輯：魯仲連 黃詩芬
美 編/插 畫：林俐
作　者：珍奈特・卡樂（Janet Cullup）
譯　者：樸慧芳
行銷部：楊伯江 朱慧娟
出版發行：高談文化事業有限公司
編輯部：台北縣新店市寶橋路235巷131號2樓之1
電　話：(02) 8919-1535
傳　真：(02) 8919-1364
E-Mail：c9728@msl6.hinet.net
印　製：久裕印刷事業股份有限公司
行政院新聞局出版事業登記證局版臺省業字第890號

霹靂龍歷險記(1)　祕密池塘
定價：450元
郵撥帳號：19282592 高談文化事業有限公司